TRANSFORMERS: MOVIE ADAPTATION ISSUE NUMBER FOUR

STORY BY ROBERTO ORCI & ALEX KURTZMAN AND JOHN ROGERS
SCREENPLAY BY ROBERTO ORCI & ALEX KURTZMAN

ADAPTATION BY KRIS OPRISKO
ART BY ALEX MILNE
COLORS BY JOSH PEREZ
WITH HELP FROM ZAC ATKINSON, JOSH BURCHAM, ANDREW ELDER, KIERAN OATS, AND ROB RUFFOLO
FLATTING ASSIST BY MARK BRISTOW AND LISA MOORE
LETTERING BY CHRIS MOWRY
EDITS BY CHRIS RYALL

Licensed by:

Special thanks to Hasbro's Aaron Archer, Elizabeth Griffin, Sheri Lucci, Richard Zambarano, Jared Jones, Michael Provost, Michael Richie, and Michael Verrecchia for their invaluable assistance.

Spotlight

IDW

DREAMWORKS PICTURES

VISIT US AT
www.abdopublishing.com

Reinforced library bound edition published in 2008 by Spotlight, a division of the ABDO Publishing Group, 8000 West 78th Street, Edina, Minnesota 55439. Published by agreement with IDW Publishing. www.idwpublishing.com

Library of Congress Cataloging-in-Publication Data

Oprisko, Kris.
Transformers : official movie adaptation / story by Roberto Orci & Alex Kurtzman and John Rogers ; screenplay by Roberto Orci & Alex Kurtzman ; adaptation by Kris Oprisko ; art by Alex Milne ; colors by Josh Perez ; color assist by Lisa Moore ; edits by Chris Ryall. -- Reinforced library bound ed.
p. cm.
ISBN 978-1-59961-481-6 (v. 1) -- ISBN 978-1-59961-482-3 (v. 2) -- ISBN 978-1-59961-483-0 (v. 3) -- ISBN 978-1-59961-484-7 (v. 4)
1. Graphic novels. I. Milne, Alex. II. Ryall, Chris. III. Transformers (Motion picture : 2007) IV. Title.

PN6727.O67T73 2008
741.5'973--dc22

2007033989

All Spotlight books have reinforced library bindings and are manufactured in the United States of America.

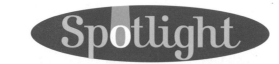

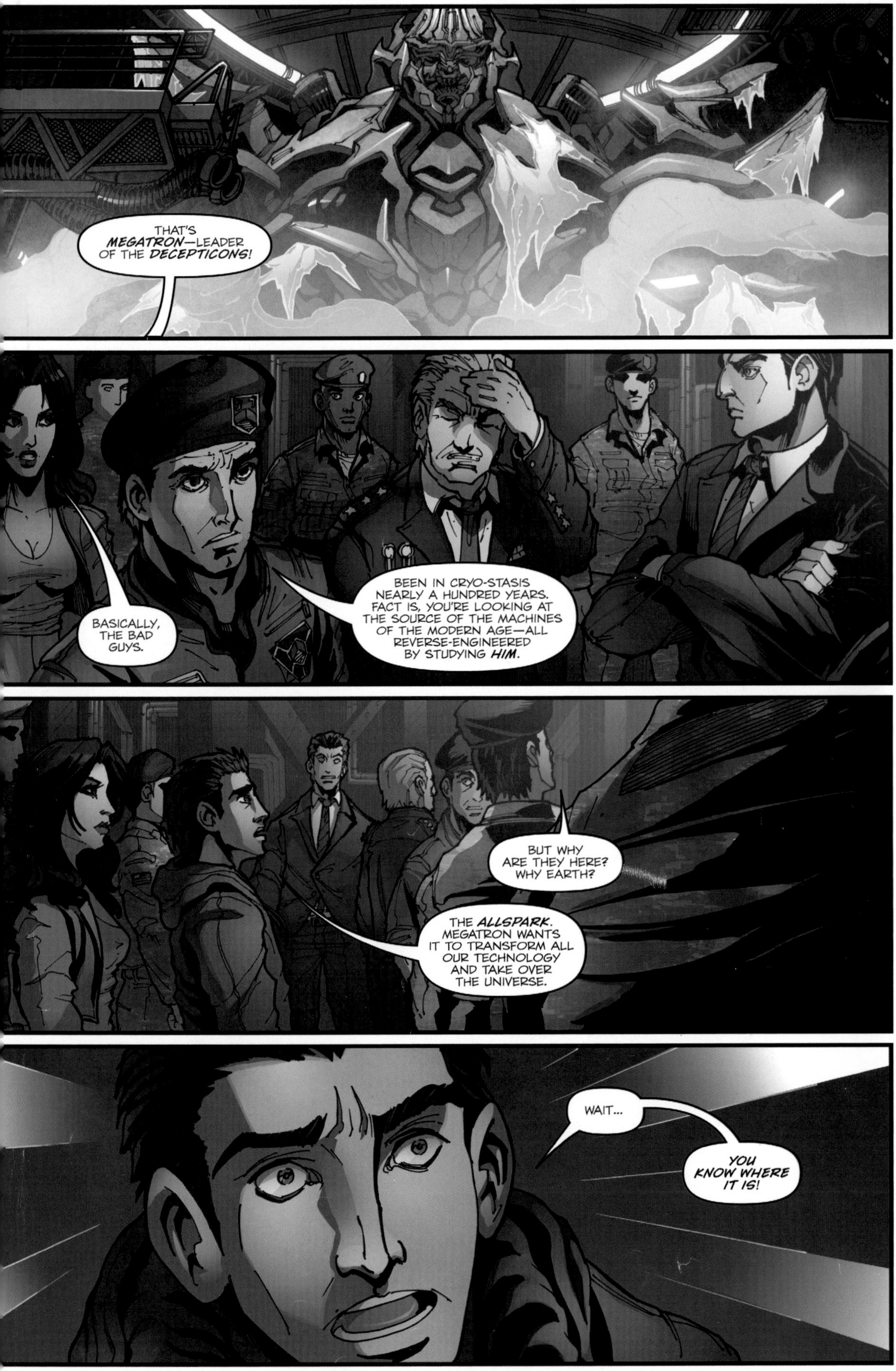
THAT'S MEGATRON—LEADER OF THE DECEPTICONS!
BASICALLY, THE BAD GUYS.
BEEN IN CRYO-STASIS NEARLY A HUNDRED YEARS. FACT IS, YOU'RE LOOKING AT THE SOURCE OF THE MACHINES OF THE MODERN AGE—ALL REVERSE-ENGINEERED BY STUDYING HIM.
BUT WHY ARE THEY HERE? WHY EARTH?
THE ALLSPARK. MEGATRON WANTS IT TO TRANSFORM ALL OUR TECHNOLOGY AND TAKE OVER THE UNIVERSE.
WAIT...
YOU KNOW WHERE IT IS!

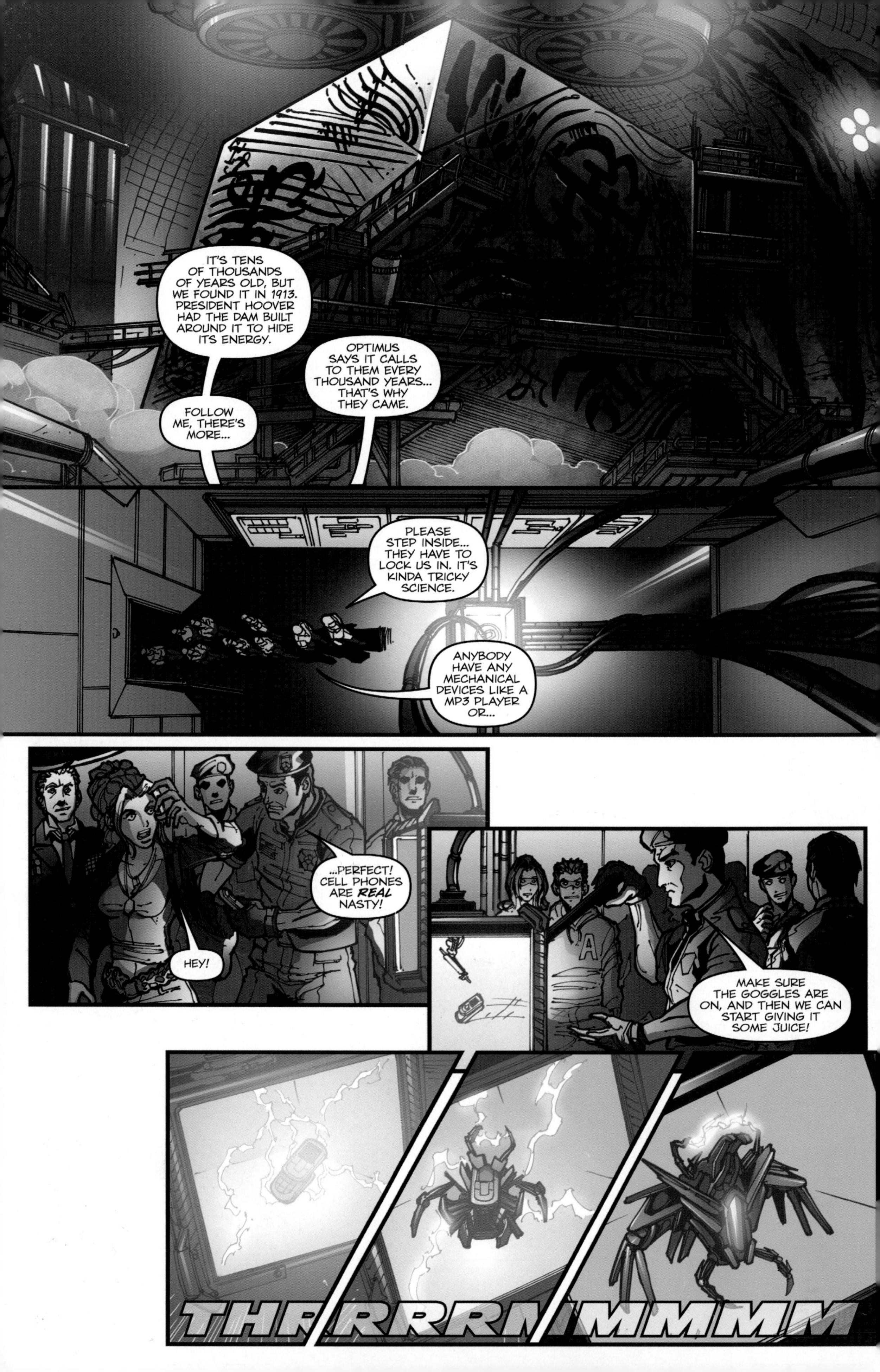
IT'S TENS OF THOUSANDS OF YEARS OLD, BUT WE FOUND IT IN 1913. PRESIDENT HOOVER HAD THE DAM BUILT AROUND IT TO HIDE ITS ENERGY.
OPTIMUS SAYS IT CALLS TO THEM EVERY THOUSAND YEARS... THAT'S WHY THEY CAME.
FOLLOW ME, THERE'S MORE...
PLEASE STEP INSIDE... THEY HAVE TO LOCK US IN. IT'S KINDA TRICKY SCIENCE.
ANYBODY HAVE ANY MECHANICAL DEVICES LIKE A MP3 PLAYER OR...
...PERFECT! CELL PHONES ARE *REAL* NASTY!
HEY!
MAKE SURE THE GOGGLES ARE ON, AND THEN WE CAN START GIVING IT SOME JUICE!
THRRRRMMMMMM

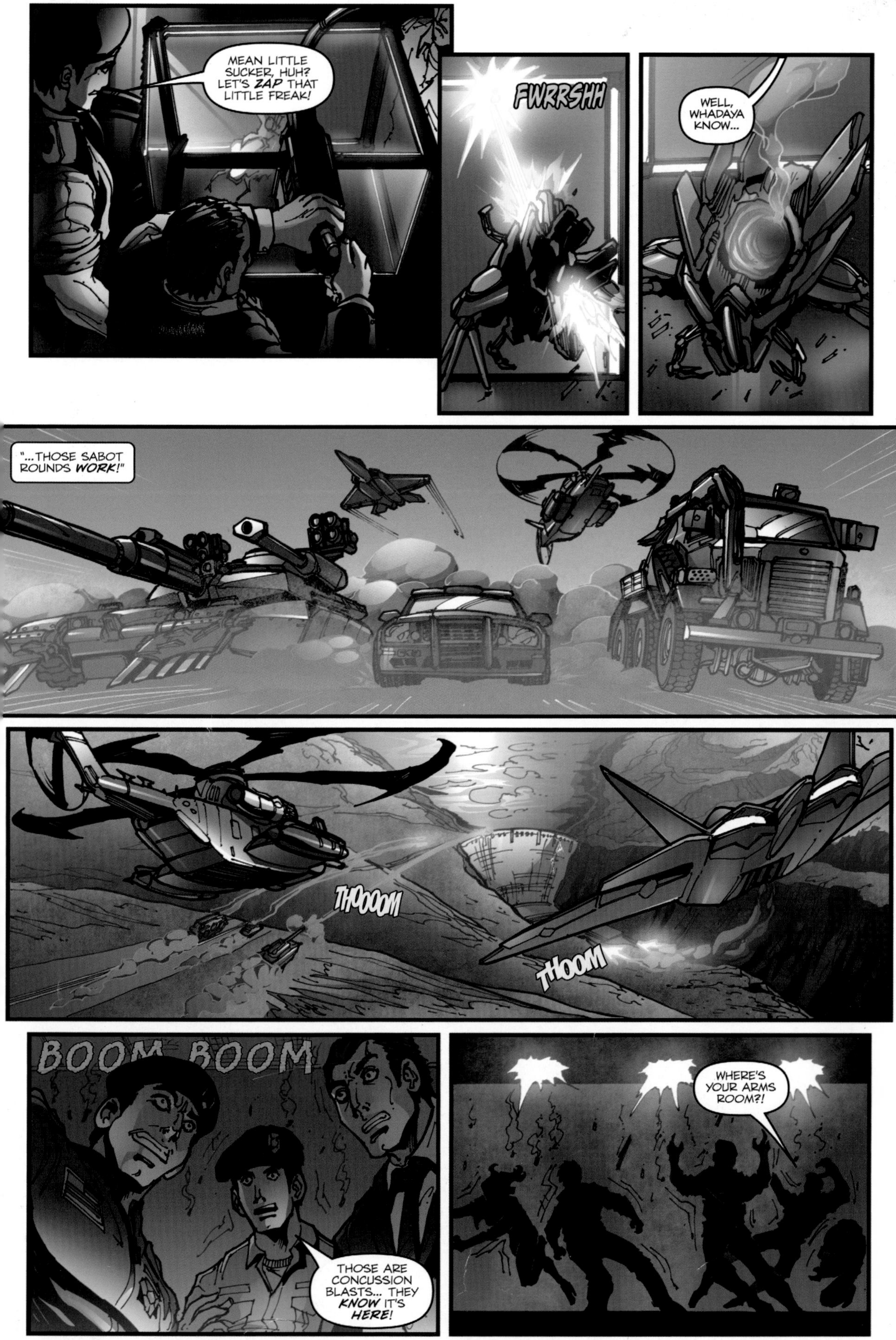
MEAN LITTLE SUCKER, HUH? LET'S ZAP THAT LITTLE FREAK!
FWRRSHH
WELL, WHADAYA KNOW...
"...THOSE SABOT ROUNDS WORK!"
THOOOOM
THOOM
BOOM BOOM
THOSE ARE CONCUSSION BLASTS... THEY KNOW IT'S HERE!
WHERE'S YOUR ARMS ROOM?!

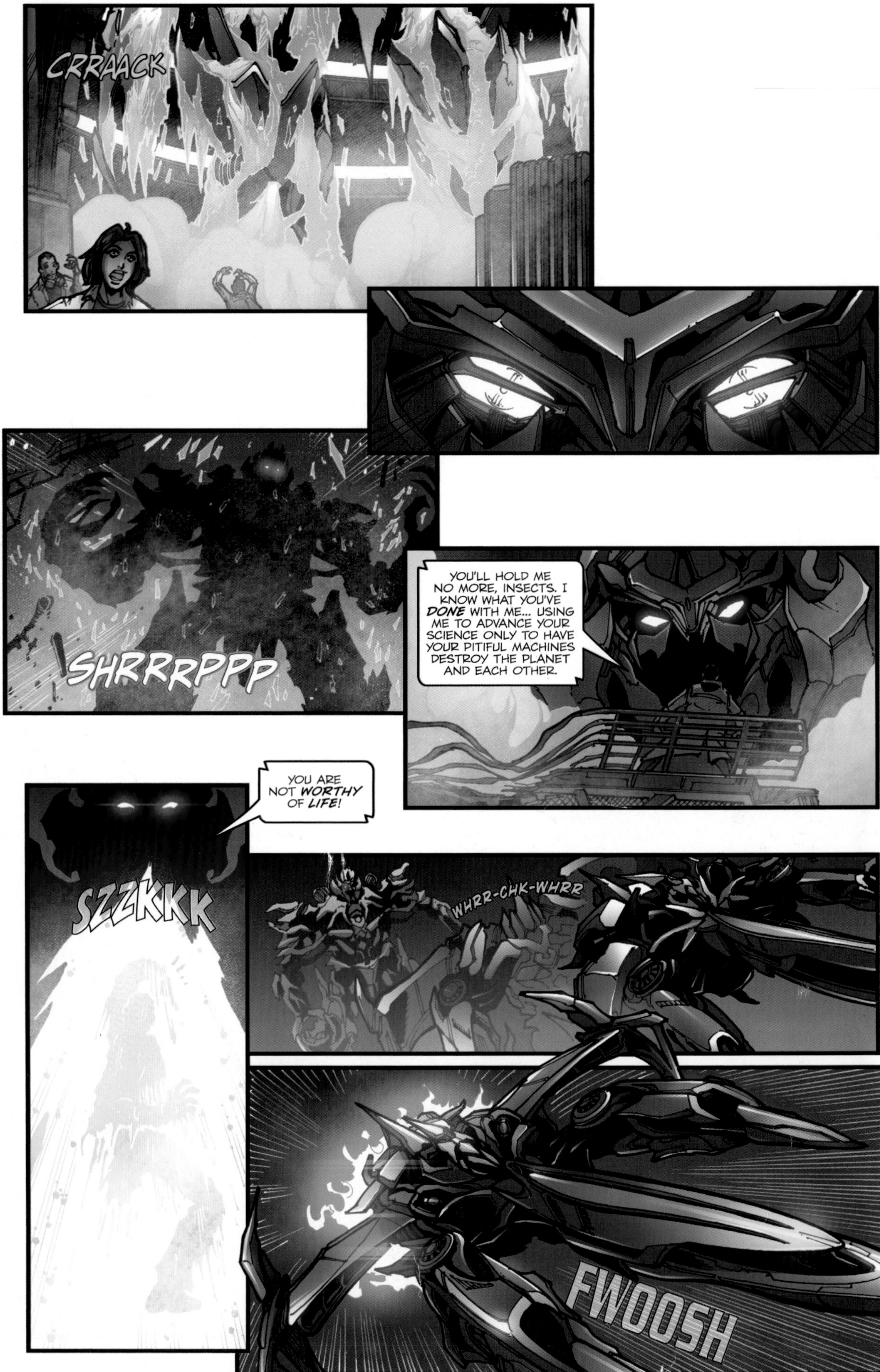
CRRAACK
SHRRRPPPP
YOU'LL HOLD ME NO MORE, INSECTS. I KNOW WHAT YOU'VE DONE WITH ME... USING ME TO ADVANCE YOUR SCIENCE ONLY TO HAVE YOUR PITIFUL MACHINES DESTROY THE PLANET AND EACH OTHER.
YOU ARE NOT WORTHY OF LIFE!
SZZKKK
WHRR-CHK-WHRR
FWOOSH

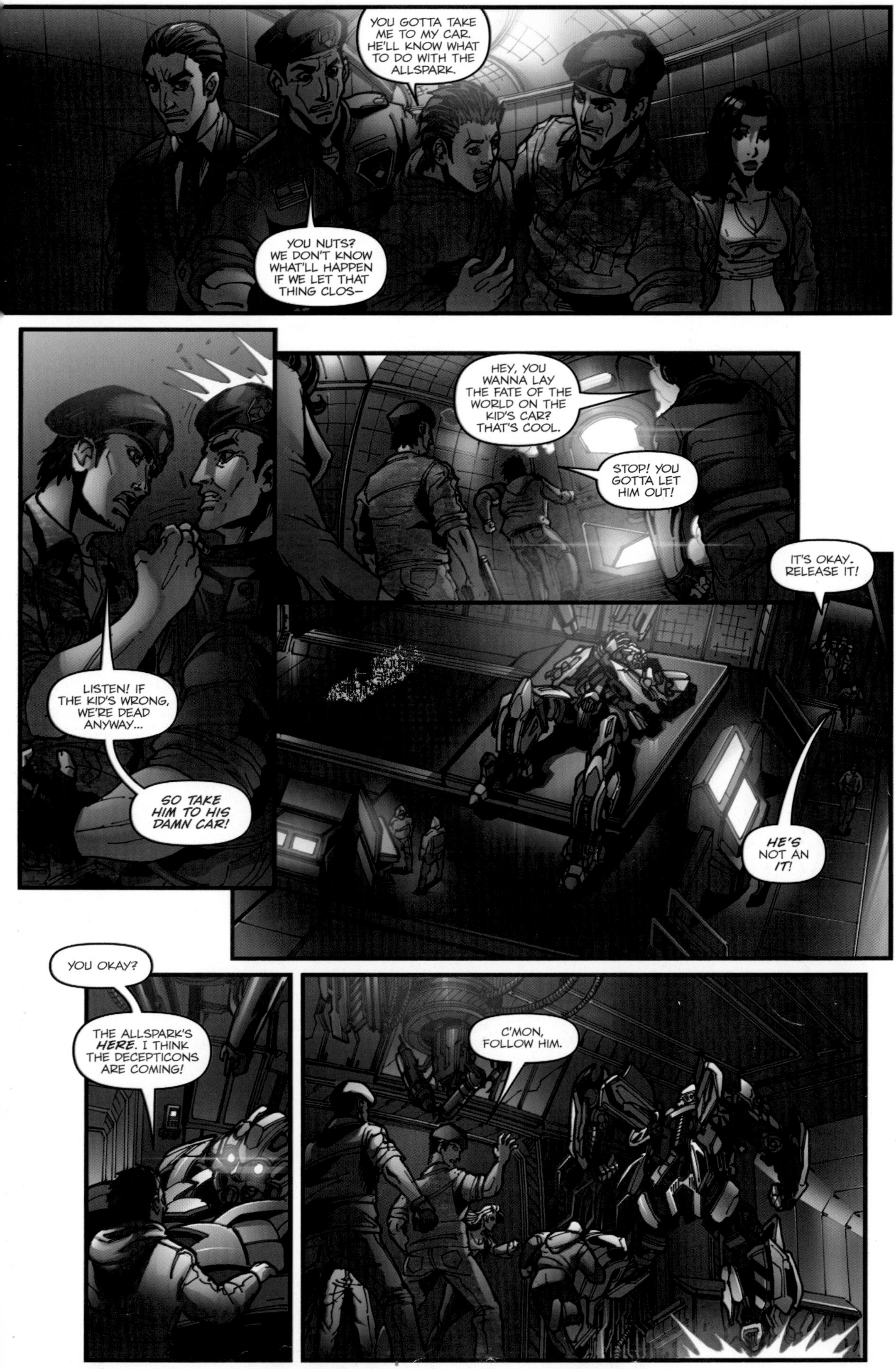
YOU GOTTA TAKE ME TO MY CAR. HE'LL KNOW WHAT TO DO WITH THE ALLSPARK.
YOU NUTS? WE DON'T KNOW WHAT'LL HAPPEN IF WE LET THAT THING CLOS—
HEY, YOU WANNA LAY THE FATE OF THE WORLD ON THE KID'S CAR? THAT'S COOL.
STOP! YOU GOTTA LET HIM OUT!
LISTEN! IF THE KID'S WRONG, WE'RE DEAD ANYWAY...
SO TAKE HIM TO HIS DAMN CAR!
IT'S OKAY. RELEASE IT!
HE'S NOT AN IT!
YOU OKAY?
THE ALLSPARK'S HERE. I THINK THE DECEPTICONS ARE COMING!
C'MON, FOLLOW HIM.

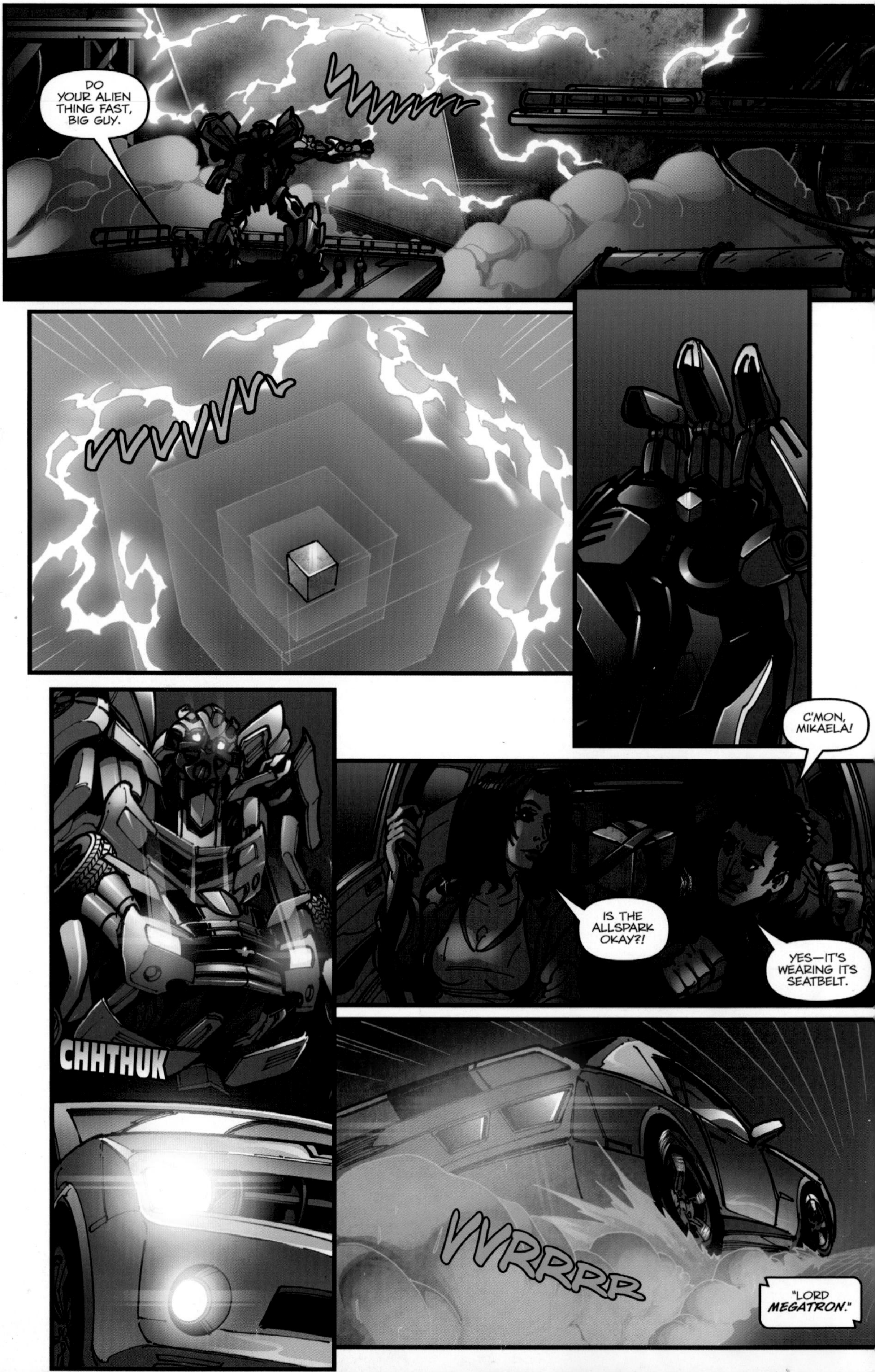
DO YOUR ALIEN THING FAST, BIG GUY.
VVVVVVVV
VVVVVVVV
C'MON, MIKAELA!
IS THE ALLSPARK OKAY?!
YES—IT'S WEARING ITS SEATBELT.
CHHTHUK
VVRRRR
"LORD MEGATRON."

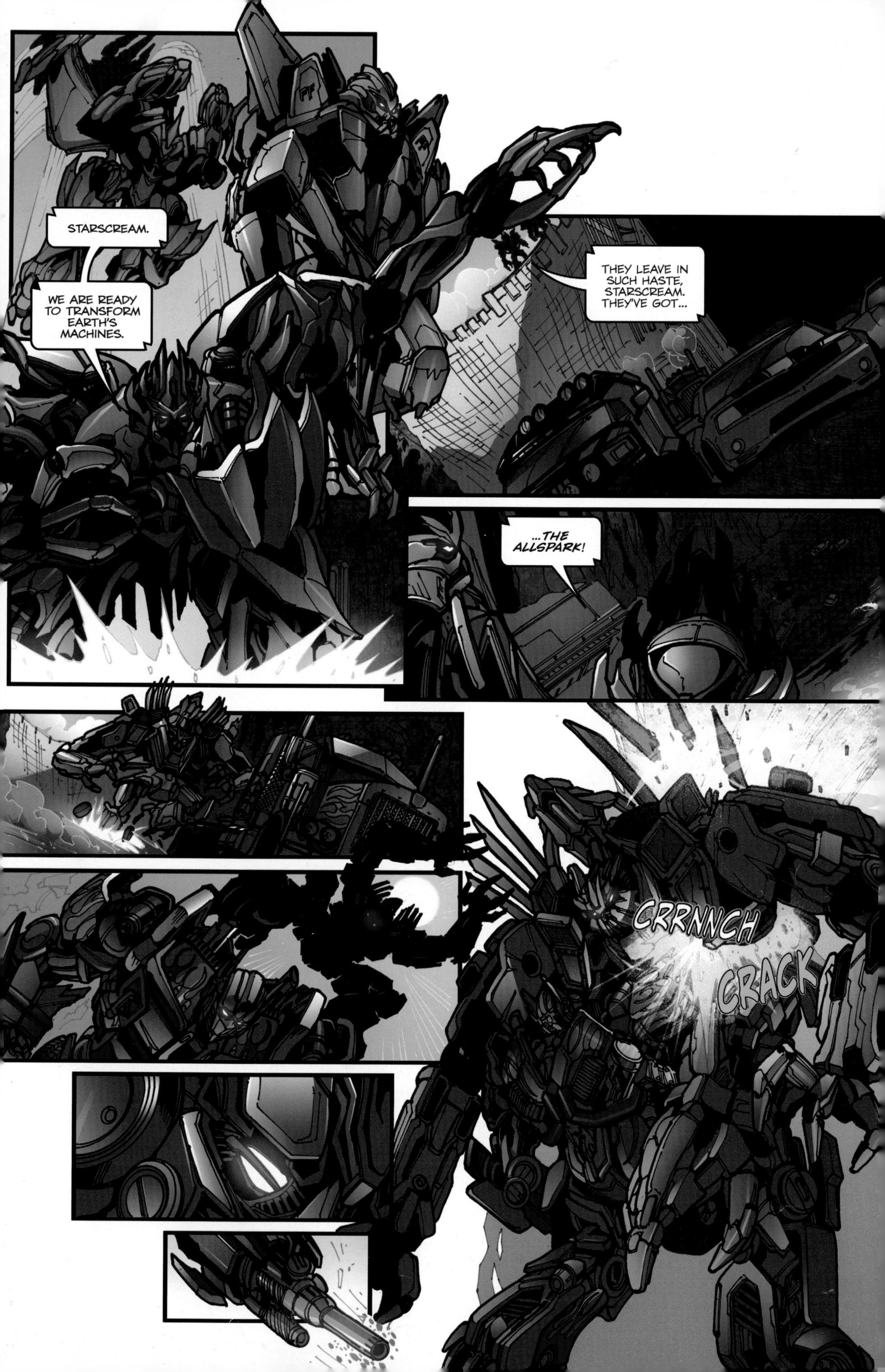

STARSCREAM.
WE ARE READY TO TRANSFORM EARTH'S MACHINES.
THEY LEAVE IN SUCH HASTE, STARSCREAM. THEY'VE GOT...
...THE ALLSPARK!
CRRNNCH
CRACK

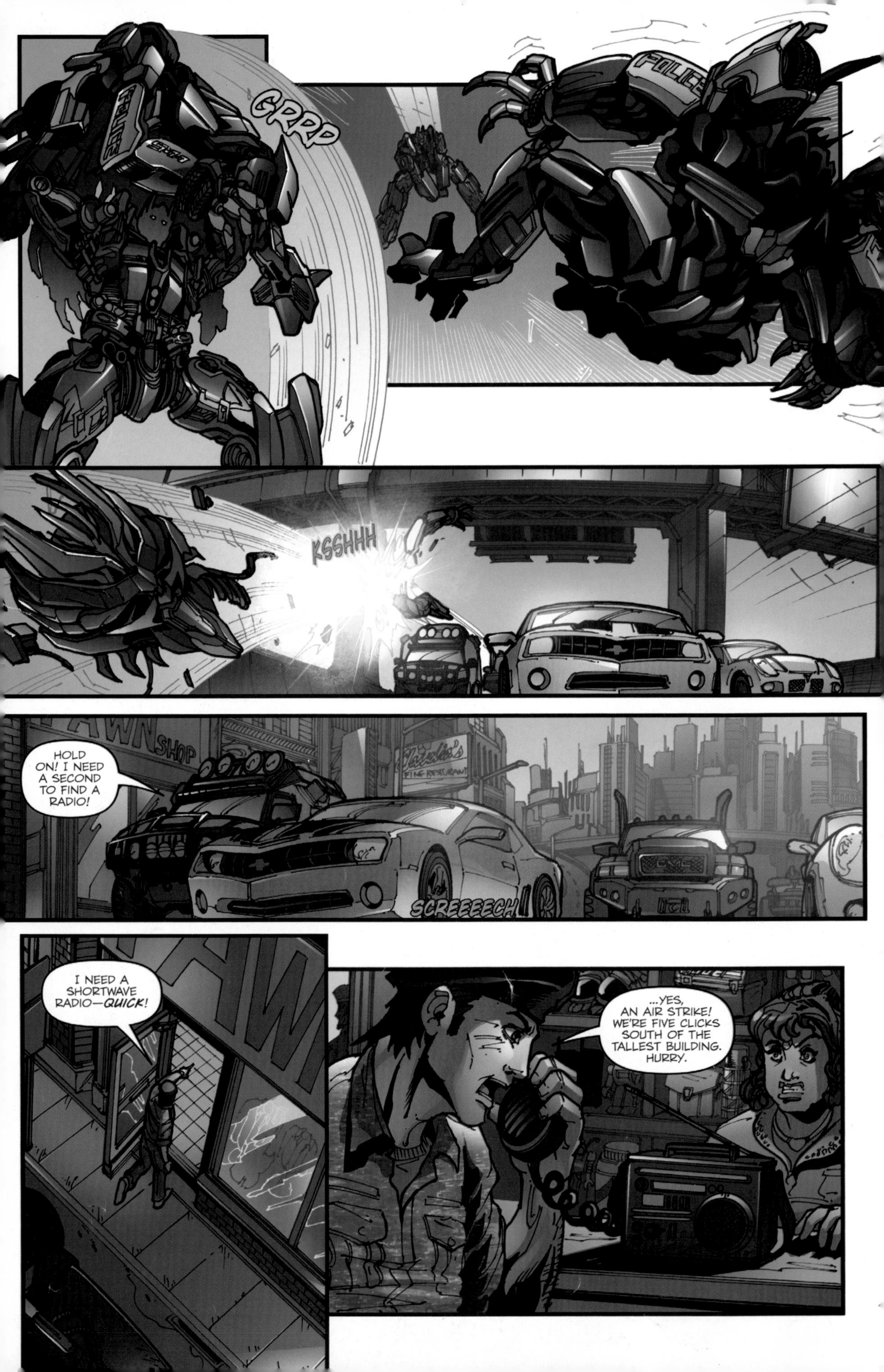
GRRP
KSSHHH
SHOP
FINE RESTURANT
HOLD ON! I NEED A SECOND TO FIND A RADIO!
SCREEEECH
I NEED A SHORTWAVE RADIO—*QUICK*!
...YES, AN AIR STRIKE! WE'RE FIVE CLICKS SOUTH OF THE TALLEST BUILDING. HURRY.

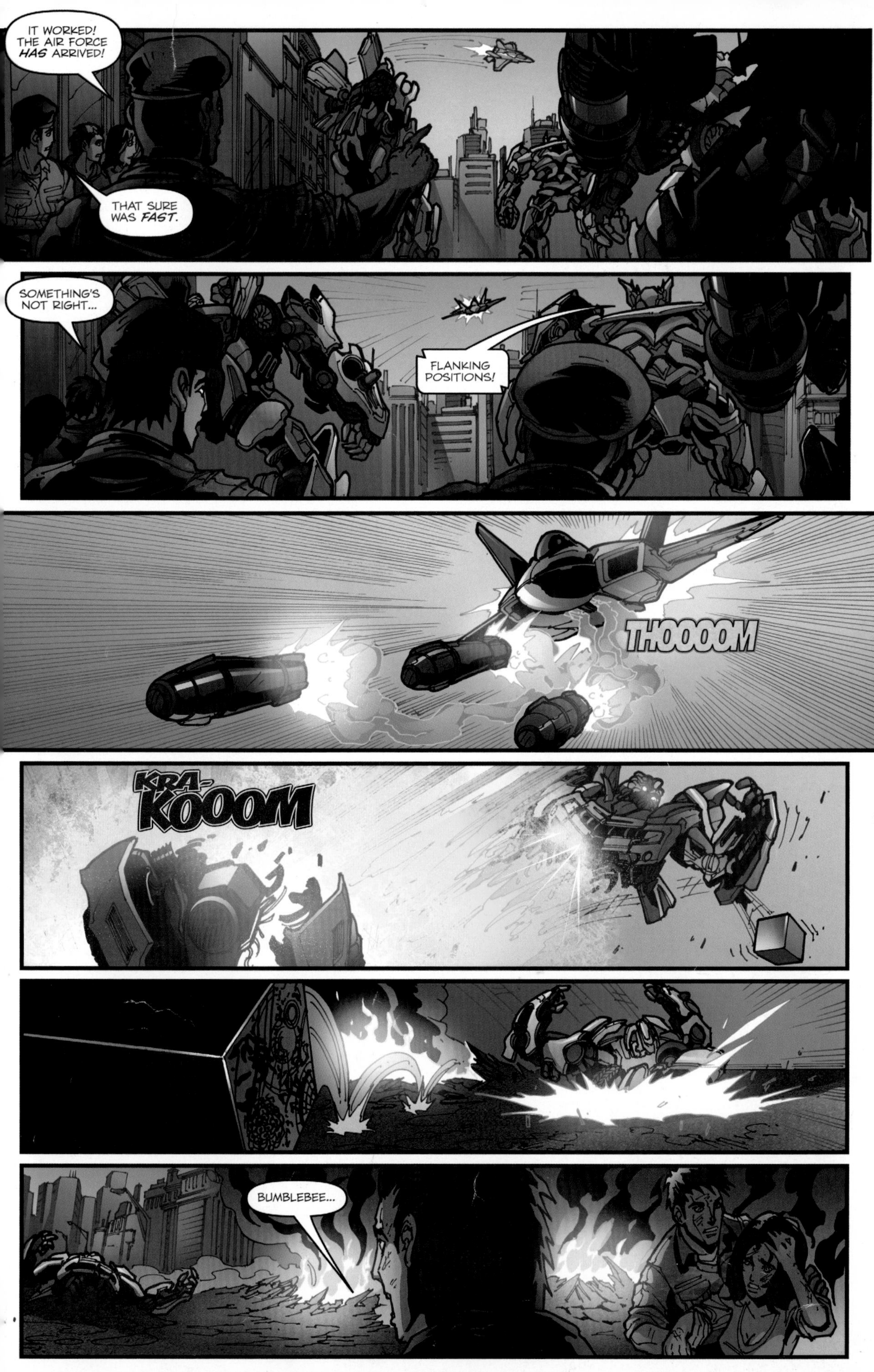
IT WORKED! THE AIR FORCE HAS ARRIVED!
THAT SURE WAS FAST.
SOMETHING'S NOT RIGHT...
FLANKING POSITIONS!
THOOOOM
KRA-KOOOM
BUMBLEBEE...

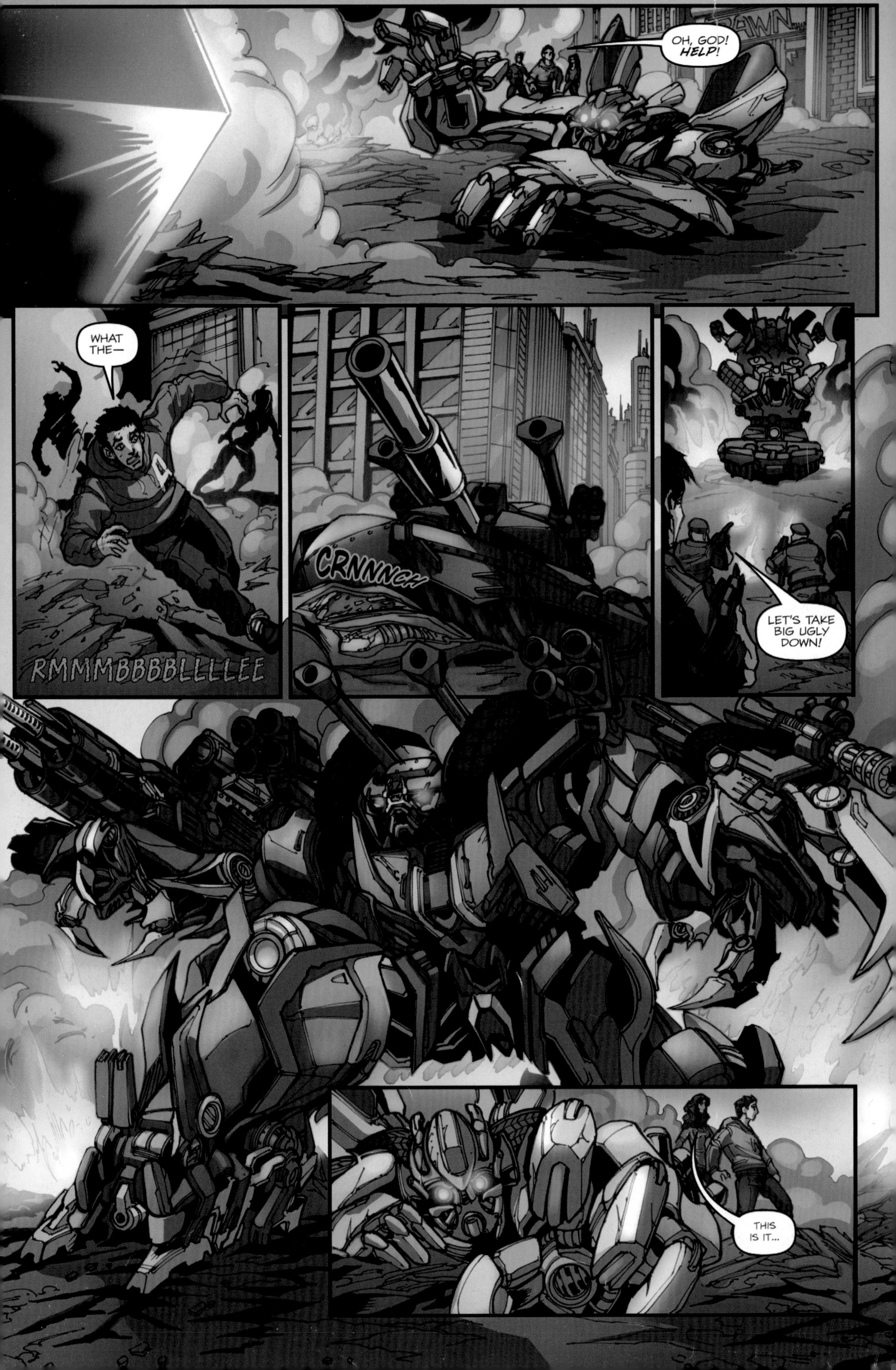
OH, GOD! **HELP!**
WHAT THE—
RMMMBBBBLLLLEE
CRNNNCH
LET'S TAKE BIG UGLY DOWN!
THIS IS IT...

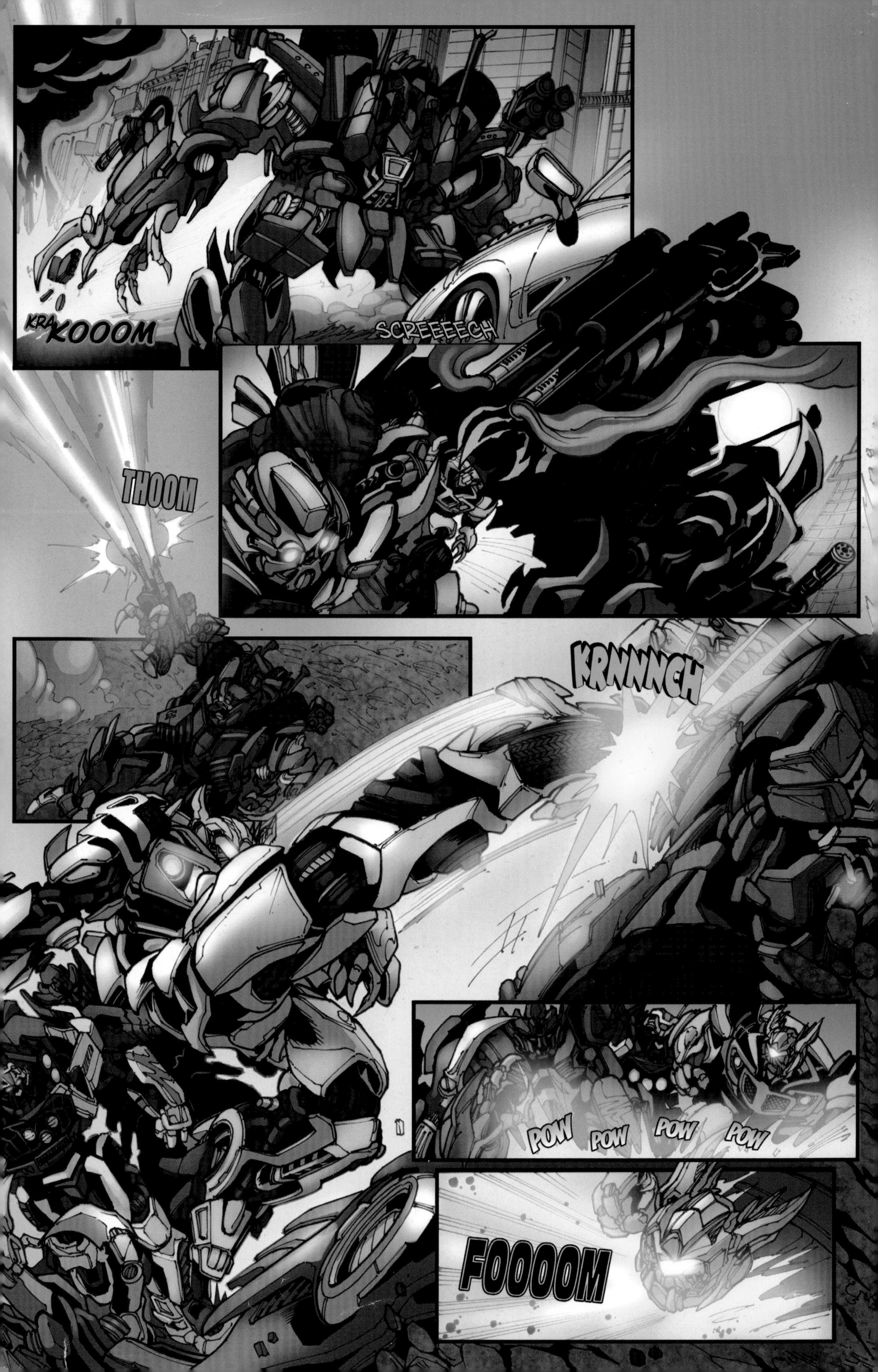
KRA-KOOOM
SCREEEEECH
THOOM
KRNNNCH
POW POW POW POW
FOOOOM

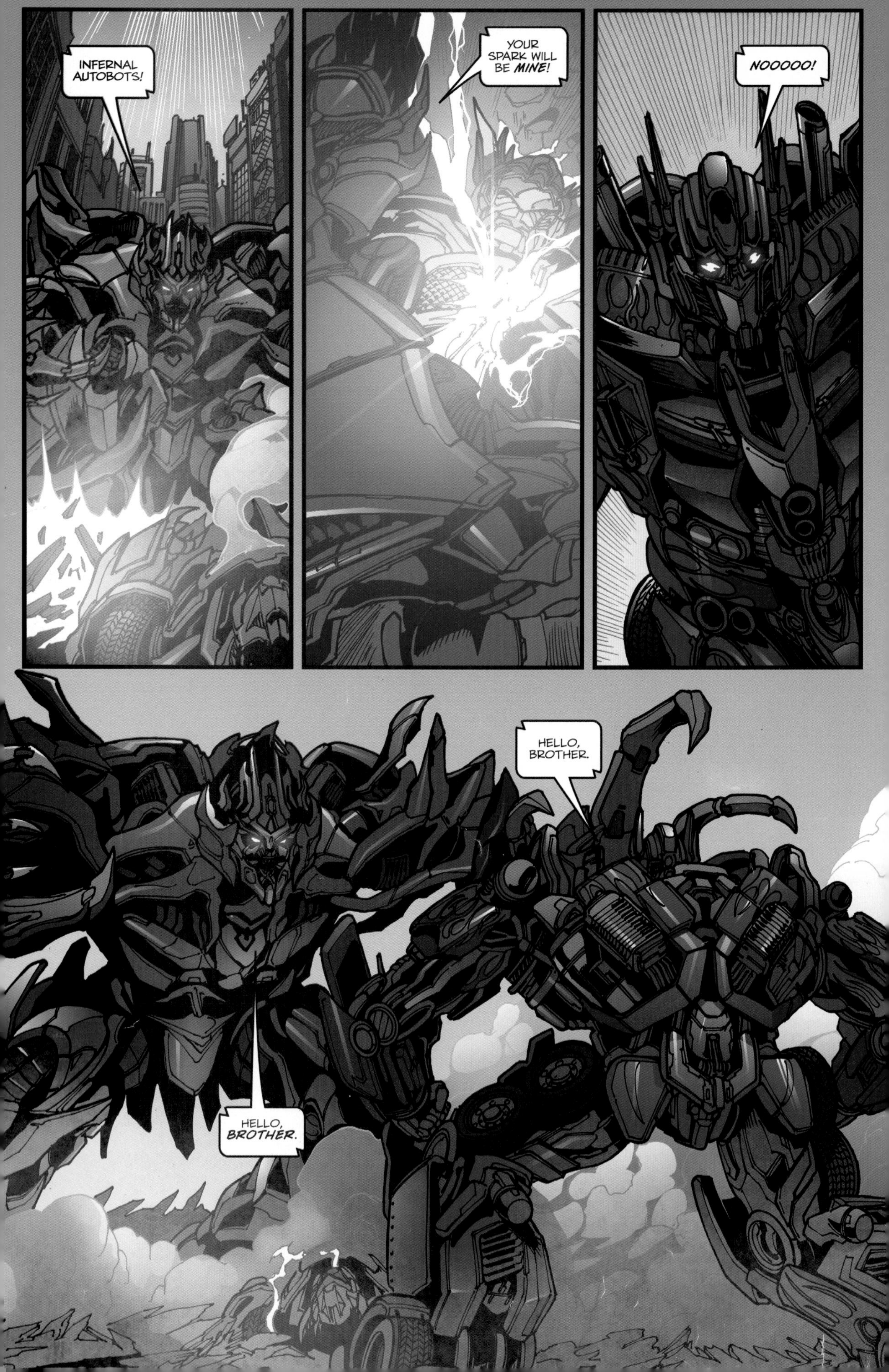
INFERNAL AUTOBOTS!
YOUR SPARK WILL BE MINE!
NOOOOO!
HELLO, BROTHER.
HELLO, BROTHER.

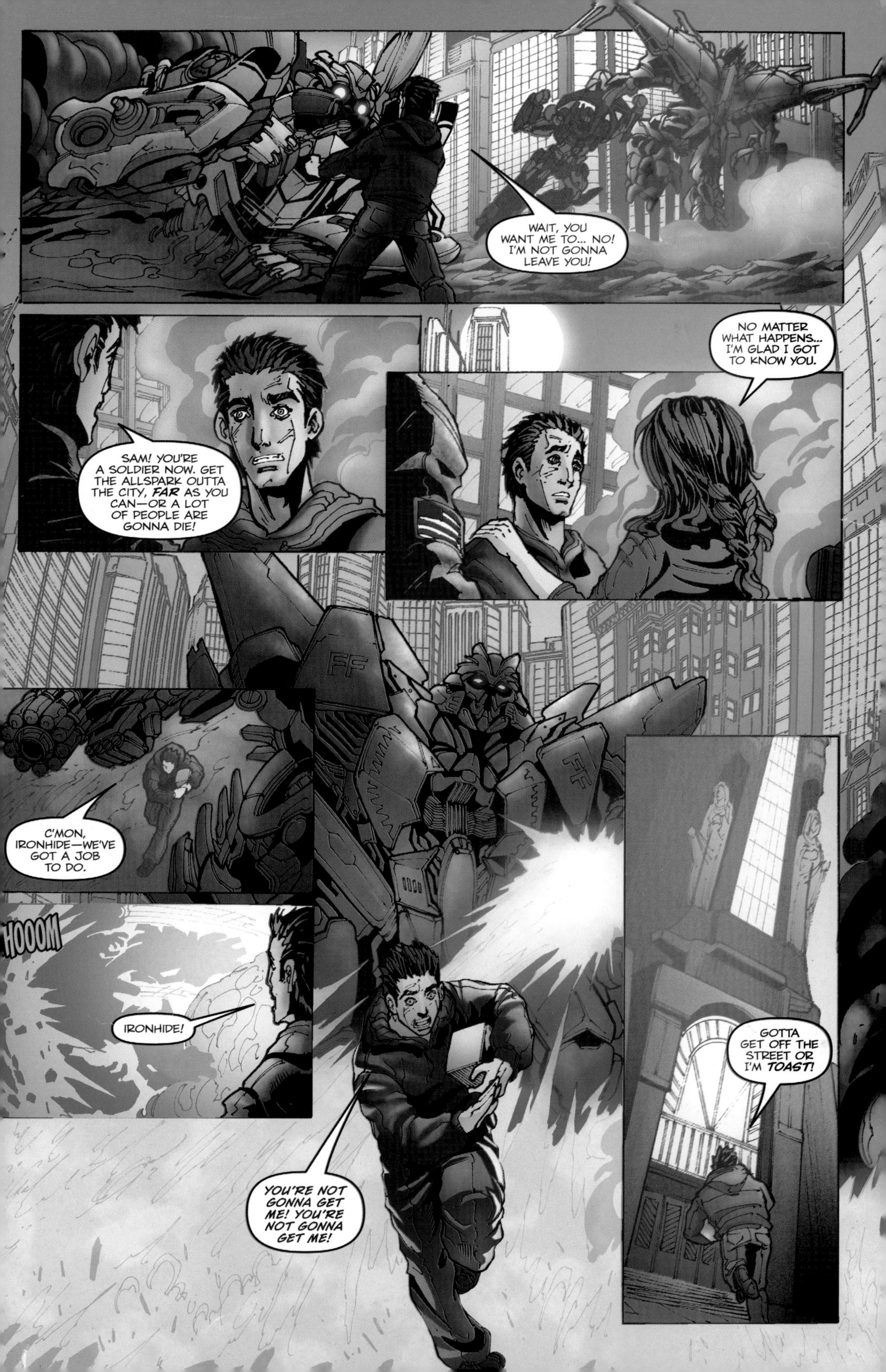
WAIT, YOU WANT ME TO... NO! I'M NOT GONNA LEAVE YOU!
SAM! YOU'RE A SOLDIER NOW. GET THE ALLSPARK OUTTA THE CITY, FAR AS YOU CAN—OR A LOT OF PEOPLE ARE GONNA DIE!
NO MATTER WHAT HAPPENS... I'M GLAD I GOT TO KNOW YOU.
C'MON, IRONHIDE—WE'VE GOT A JOB TO DO.
HOOOM
IRONHIDE!
YOU'RE NOT GONNA GET ME! YOU'RE NOT GONNA GET ME!
GOTTA GET OFF THE STREET OR I'M TOAST!

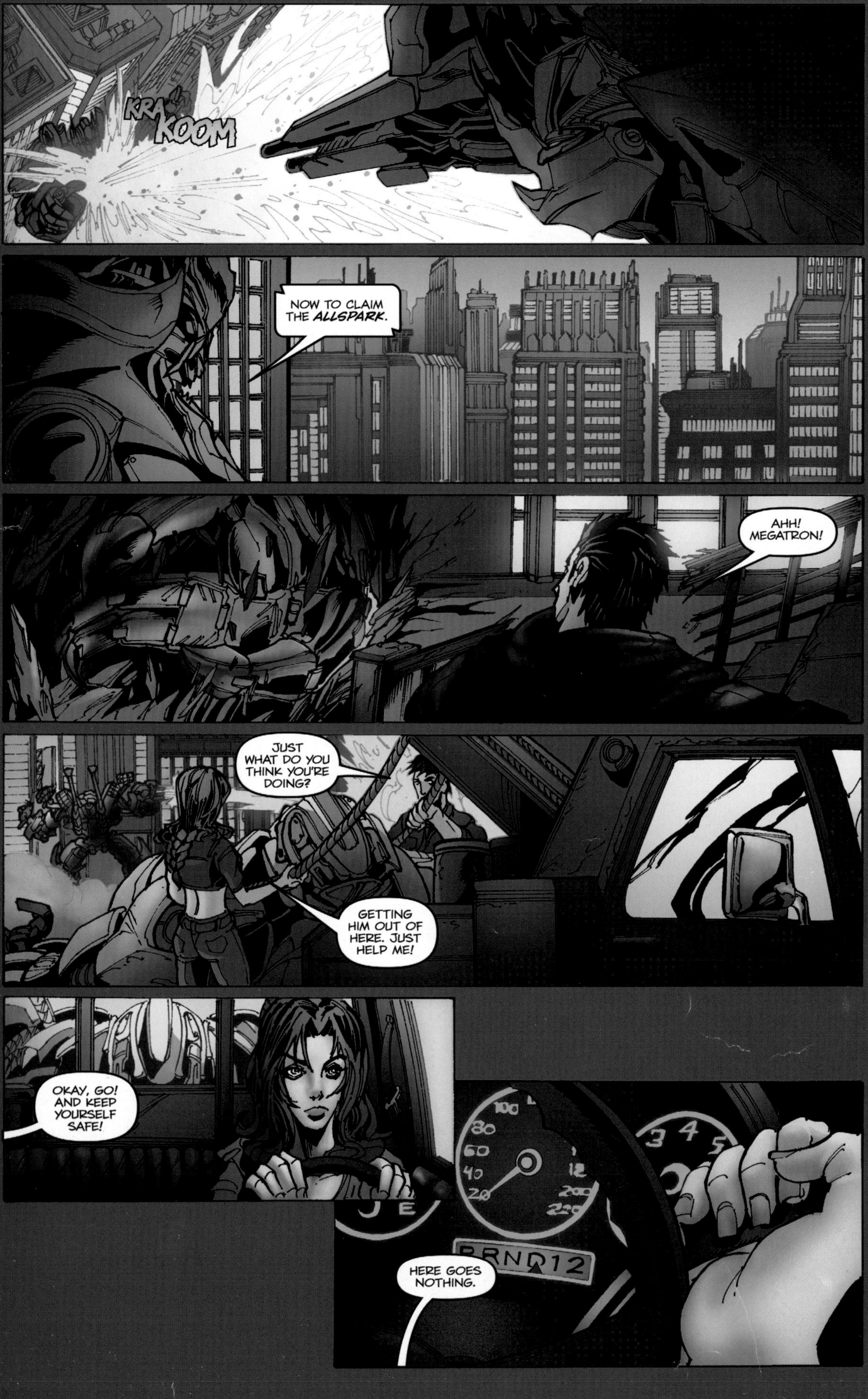
KRA-KOOM
NOW TO CLAIM THE ALLSPARK.
AHH! MEGATRON!
JUST WHAT DO YOU THINK YOU'RE DOING?
GETTING HIM OUT OF HERE. JUST HELP ME!
OKAY, GO! AND KEEP YOURSELF SAFE!
PRND12
HERE GOES NOTHING.

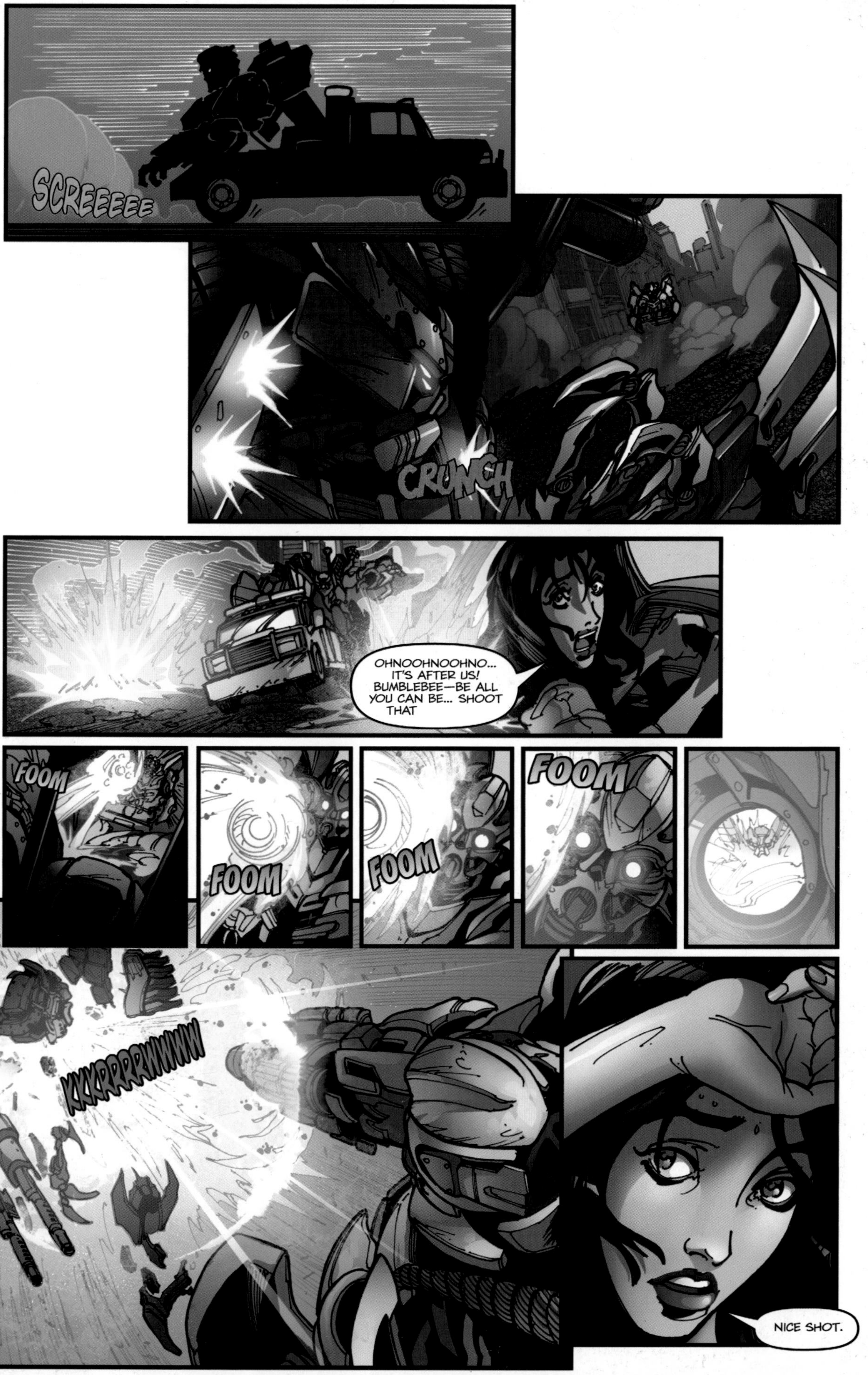
SCREEEEEE
CRUNCH
OHNOOHNOOHNO... IT'S AFTER US! BUMBLEBEE—BE ALL YOU CAN BE... SHOOT THAT
FOOM
FOOM
FOOM
FOOM
KKKRRRRWWWW
NICE SHOT.

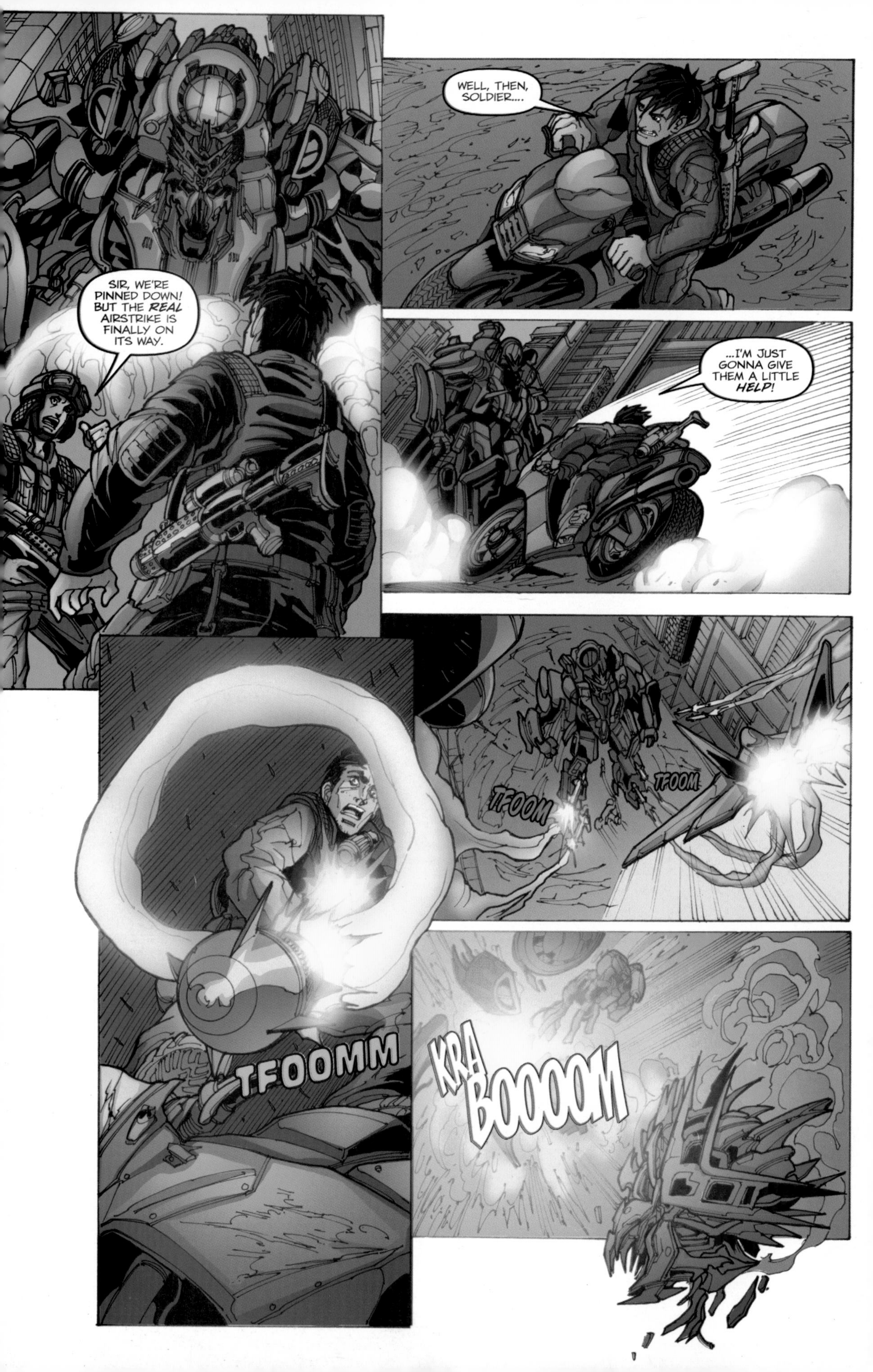
SIR, WE'RE PINNED DOWN! BUT THE REAL AIRSTRIKE IS FINALLY ON ITS WAY.
WELL, THEN, SOLDIER....
...I'M JUST GONNA GIVE THEM A LITTLE HELP!
TFOOMM
TFOOM
TFOOM
KRA BOOOOM

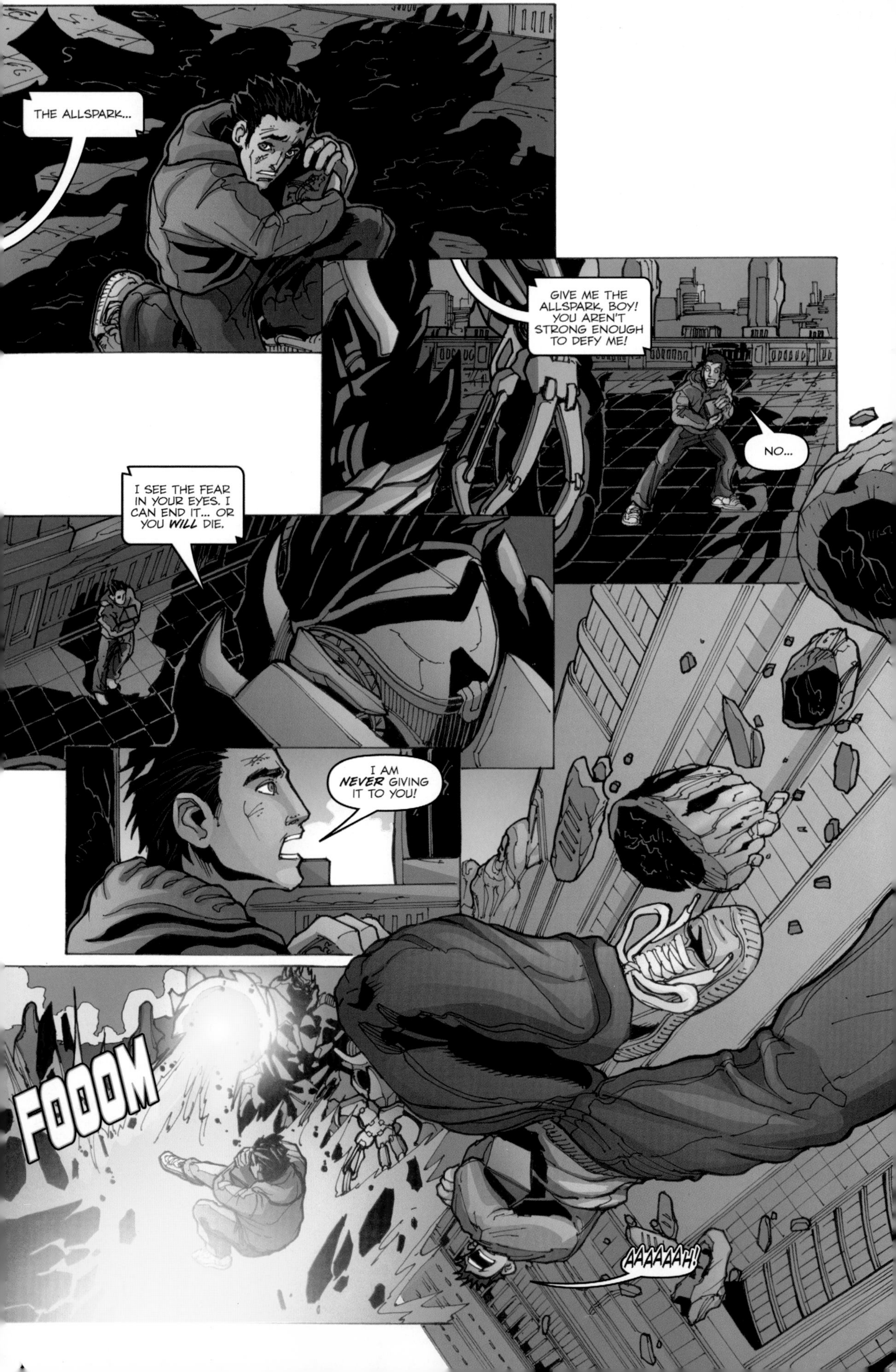

THE ALLSPARK...
GIVE ME THE ALLSPARK, BOY! YOU AREN'T STRONG ENOUGH TO DEFY ME!
NO...
I SEE THE FEAR IN YOUR EYES. I CAN END IT... OR YOU *WILL* DIE.
I AM *NEVER* GIVING IT TO YOU!
FOOOM
AAAAAAH!

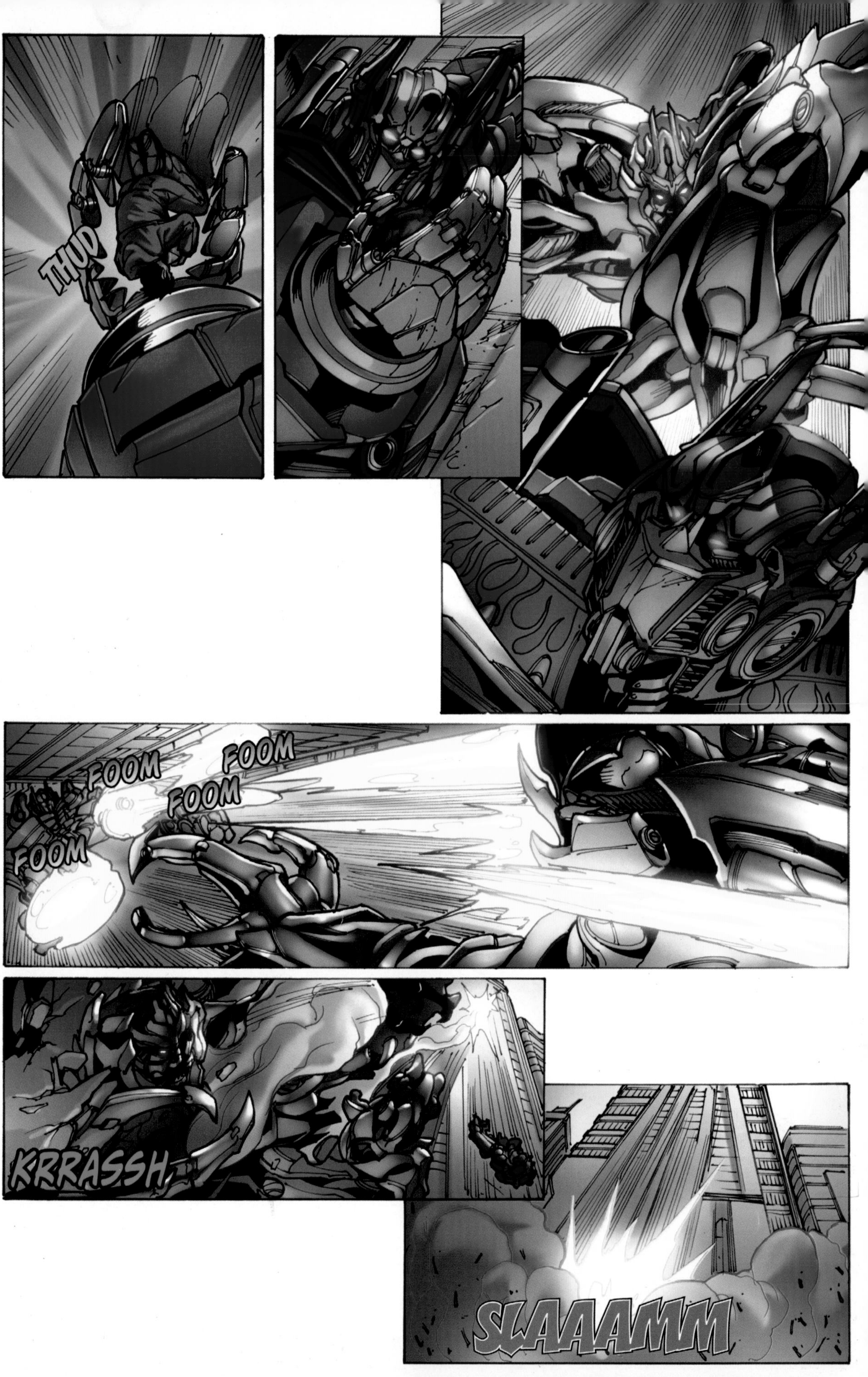
THUD
FOOM
FOOM
FOOM
FOOM
KRRASSH
SLAAAMM

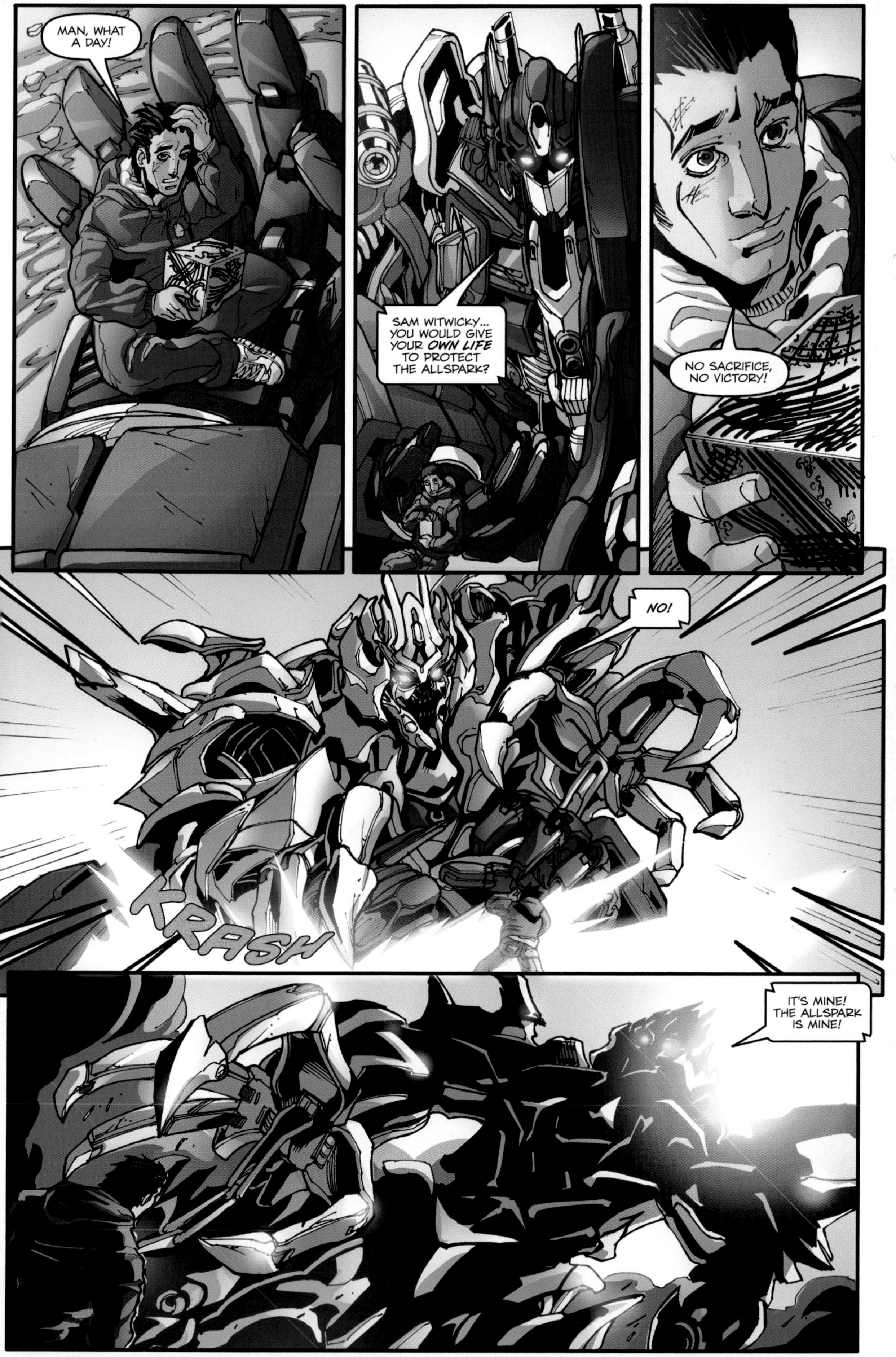
MAN, WHAT A DAY!
SAM WITWICKY... YOU WOULD GIVE YOUR OWN LIFE TO PROTECT THE ALLSPARK?
NO SACRIFICE, NO VICTORY!
NO!
KRASH
IT'S MINE! THE ALLSPARK IS MINE!

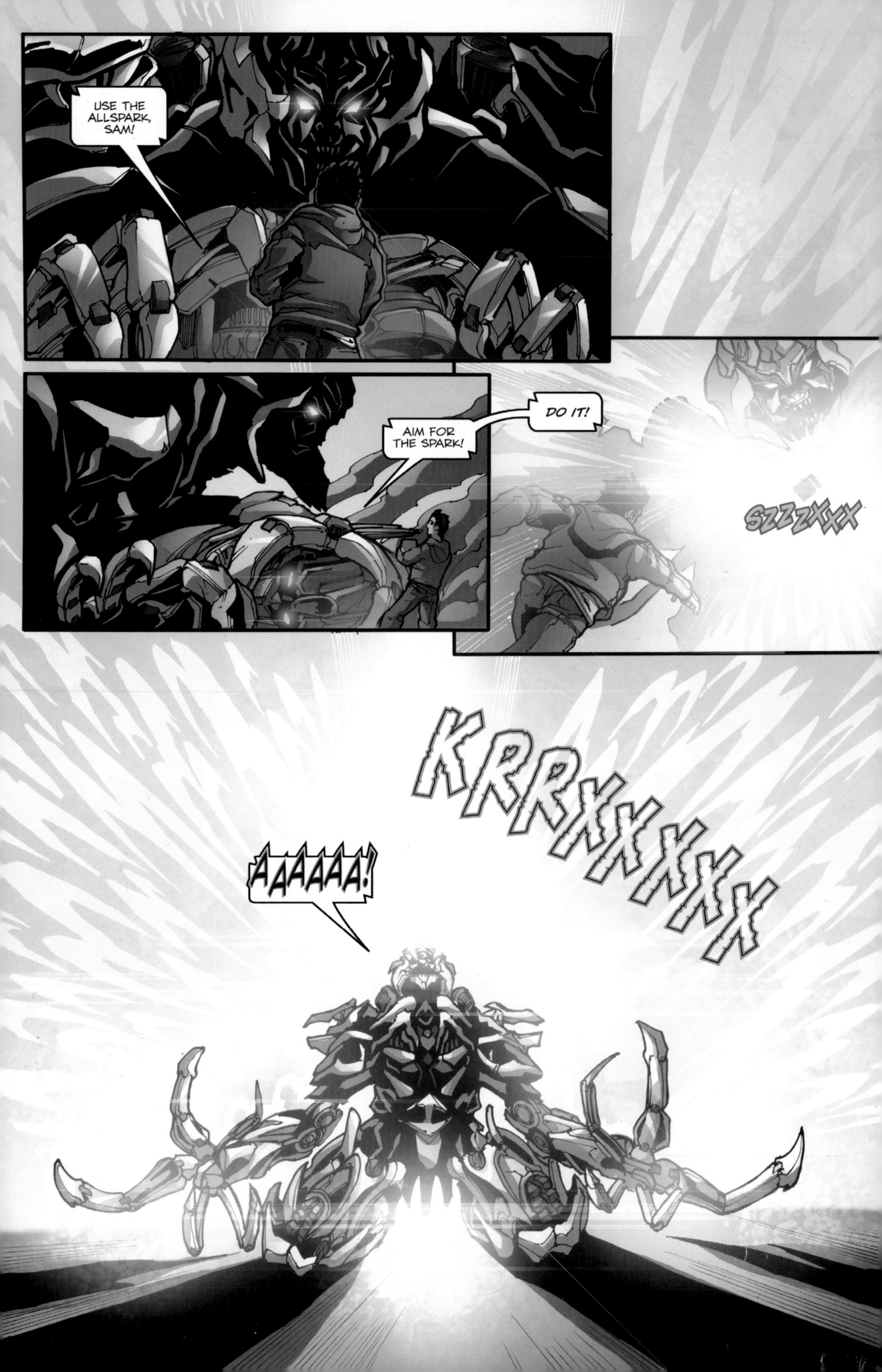
USE THE ALLSPARK, SAM!
AIM FOR THE SPARK!
DO IT!
SZZZXXX
KRRXXXXXX
AAAAAA!

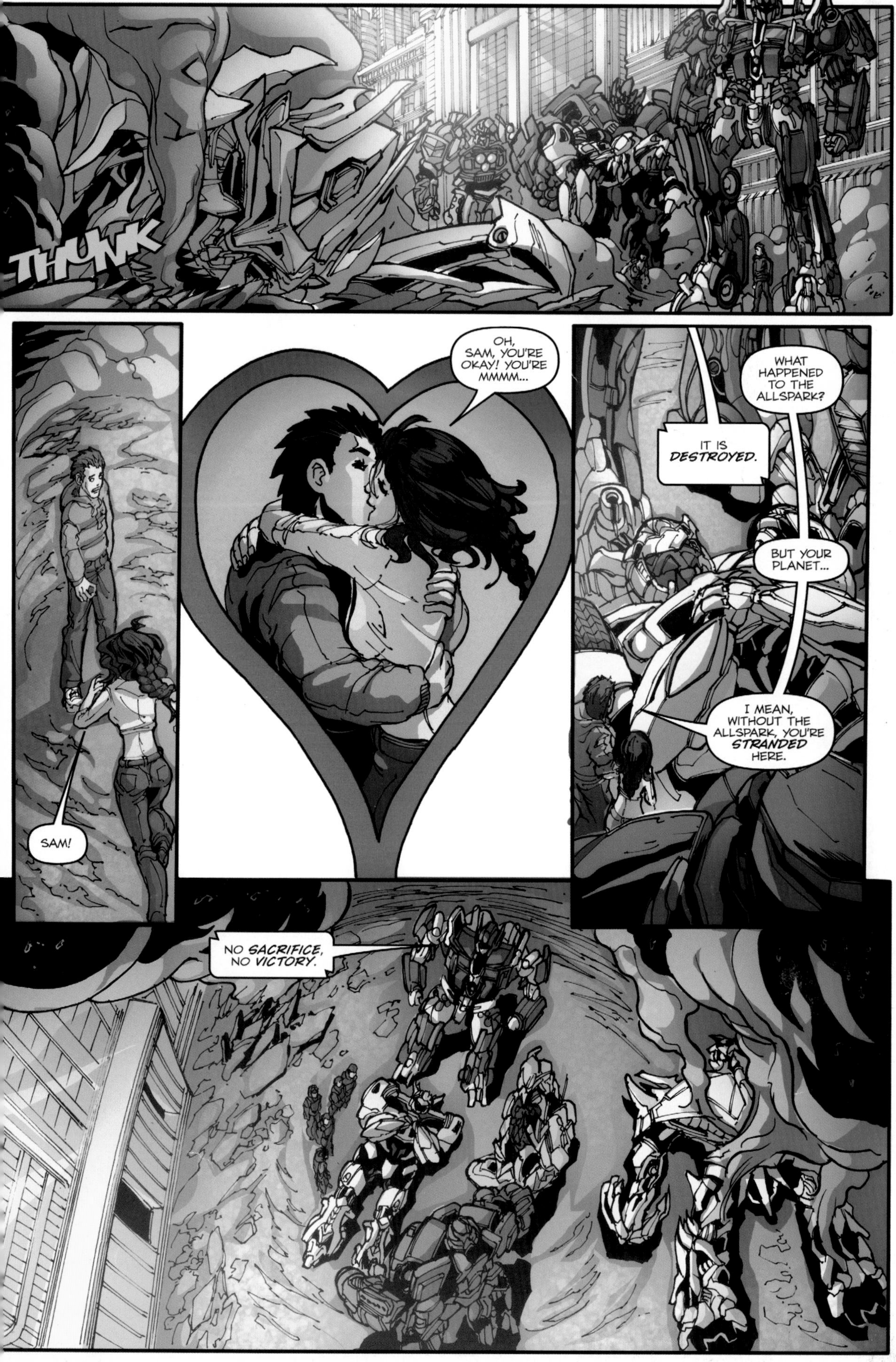
THUNK
SAM!
OH, SAM, YOU'RE OKAY! YOU'RE MMMM...
WHAT HAPPENED TO THE ALLSPARK?
IT IS DESTROYED.
BUT YOUR PLANET...
I MEAN, WITHOUT THE ALLSPARK, YOU'RE STRANDED HERE.
NO SACRIFICE, NO VICTORY.

IN AN EFFORT TO LIMIT AWARENESS OF THE SITUATION, SECTOR SEVEN HAS BEEN TERMINATED—AND THE REMAINS OF THE DEAD ALIENS ARE BEING DISPOSED OF IN THE LAURENTIAN ABYSS. AT SEVEN MILES BELOW SEA LEVEL, IT'S THE DEEPEST POINT ON THE PLANET.

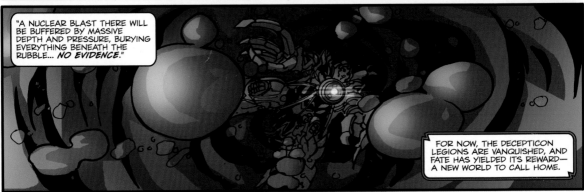

"A NUCLEAR BLAST THERE WILL BE BUFFERED BY MASSIVE DEPTH AND PRESSURE, BURYING EVERYTHING BENEATH THE RUBBLE... *NO EVIDENCE.*"

FOR NOW, THE DECEPTICON LEGIONS ARE VANQUISHED, AND FATE HAS YIELDED ITS REWARD— A NEW WORLD TO CALL HOME.

WE LIVE AMONG ITS PEOPLE NOW, HIDING IN PLAIN SIGHT... BUT WATCHING OVER THEM IN SECRET. WAITING. PROTECTING.

I HAVE WITNESSED THEIR CAPACITY FOR COURAGE. AND THOUGH WE ARE WORLDS APART, LIKE US, THERE'S *MORE TO THEM THAN MEETS THE EYE.*

I AM OPTIMUS PRIME, AND I SEND THIS MESSAGE TO ANY SURVIVING AUTOBOTS TAKING REFUGE AMONG THE STARS. YOU ARE NOT ALONE.

WE ARE HERE. WE ARE WAITING.

END.